A Puppy's First Christmas

A Puppy's First Christmas

by Holly Webb

Illustrated by Sophy Williams

SCHOLASTIC INC.

For everyone who has enjoyed this series through the years

Originally published in Great Britain in 2021 by the Little Tiger Group

ISBN 978-1-339-04332-6

12 11 10 9 8 7 6 5 4 3 2 1   23 24 25 26 27 28

Printed in the U.S.A.   40

First Scholastic printing, September 2023

Contents

Chapter One
The Start of Christmas Break

Aria slid out of the classroom door
and stood next to it, her back pressed
against the wall, breathing hard. She
had been looking forward to the end of
the quarter Christmas party—so many
games and fun and party food—but it
had all been too much. The inside of
her head seemed to be spinning around
and around, and she felt dizzy.

Suddenly, she wanted nothing more than to be back at home, curled up on the couch, with Jackson's head resting in her lap—or all of Jackson in her lap would be even better. She'd be petting her puppy's soft fur, and everything would be peaceful….

"Are you all right, Aria? I saw you come out. Are you feeling sick?" Miss Lyons popped her head around the door, looking worried.

Aria shook her head and tried to smile.

"I'm okay. It's just … really noisy. And … bright…."

"It is a lot," Miss Lyons agreed, but she still looked concerned. "It's not long until the end of school, though. In fact, we should probably start cleaning up. Would you be able to run a little errand for me? Could you go and ask Mr. Fordham if I could have my cleaning spray? He borrowed it yesterday, and I'm going to need it to wipe down all those sticky tables."

Aria was pretty sure Miss Lyons had invented the errand to give her some time away from the classroom, but she didn't mind. She nodded and walked slowly down the hallway to the third-grade classroom to find Mr. Fordham. If she was really slow, it would be practically time to go home when she got back.

What was it about the party that had been so hard to cope with? Aria wondered as she headed back up the hallway with the bottle of spray. *The noise? Everyone rushing around?* Maybe it was just the excitement that seemed to be bubbling up out of everyone because it was the end of the quarter. Aria could understand that. She loved Christmas, and she'd been excited about it forever. The last few weeks had been cold and damp and miserable, and her whole class was desperate for the holidays to come.

By the time she got back to the

classroom, the floor was covered in a thin layer of crushed-up chips and broken cookies. Everyone was helping to clean up, grumbling a little, but mostly looking forward to the bell going off and heading home for the Christmas break. Miss Lyons was already sending people off in twos and threes to get their coats.

"Thanks, Aria, I'll take that—you go and get your things."

Aria went to put her coat on, hoping that Dad would bring Jackson with him when he came to pick up her and her brother, James. For some reason, Aria had really missed Jackson today. They'd only had him for a couple of months, but now she couldn't imagine their house without a wriggling ball of chocolate Labrador puppy. Jackson was beautiful, and whenever she was tired or upset, he made her feel better. He wasn't always calm—he could be excited and bouncy and puppyish when they were out in the yard or at the park. But if Aria was feeling like things were too much, Jackson seemed to know. He'd come and lie on top of her—just when she needed the weight of him. Aria would hug him back, and all the buzzy worry in her head would drain away.

Aria hurried out onto the playground when the bell rang, waving good-bye and calling "Merry Christmas!" to her friends.

Yes! There was Dad, just outside the gate, and he had Jackson with him! The puppy was looking so sweet in his new red collar and leash, and Aria could see kids from her class giving him admiring glances. Jackson spotted her coming, and Aria smiled to herself as he started to bounce up and down, whining with excitement. It felt good that he was so happy to see her.

"Hello, love! Did you have a fun day? How was your party?" Dad asked.

Aria crouched down to rub Jackson's ears and shrugged. "It was okay…. It was a little too loud." Mom and Dad knew that she couldn't deal with noise and big groups sometimes. Things like that could make her feel weird and shaky and upset—Mom said she was more sensitive to them than other people were. Aria could tell that Dad was a little worried about her now. "I went out into the hallway for some of it."

Dad nodded. "Sounds like that was a good idea. What are you going to do when you get home? How are you starting off the holidays?"

Aria smiled at Dad. She could tell he was trying to change the subject. "I'm going to wrap up—" she pressed her hands gently over Jackson's ears— "Jackson's present! I bought it with Mom when we went shopping over the weekend. It's a special dog toy, for Jackson's first Christmas."

"Nice!" Dad nodded and then waved. "Oh, hey, James!"

Jackson squirmed lovingly around James's knees and Aria's big brother picked him up, letting Jackson lick his cheek.

"Hello! Who's a good boy?"

"We'd better head home because we have a lot of decorating to do," Dad said. "I picked up the Christmas tree this morning! Plus I'm getting chilly, and I bet Jackson is, too, since we've been standing out here for a while."

"Mr. Turner said he thinks it's going to snow soon," James said as they set off for home.

"Really? Real snow that sticks?" Aria asked excitedly. There'd been a little bit of snow back in November, but hardly enough to make a snowball, let alone a snowman.

"Yeah, he said so. I hope it snows for when Matthew's here."

Aria nodded, but she looked thoughtful. Matthew was their cousin, and he had two younger sisters, Lucy and Hannah. All three of them were coming to stay the day before Christmas Eve, with Aunt Anna, Mom's sister, and Uncle Josh. *And* Grandma and Grandpa. Aria was really looking forward to it, especially since she didn't get to see her cousins very often—they'd never even met Jackson!—but it was going to be a busy, noisy houseful. She loved the thought of a big family Christmas, but she couldn't help feeling just a little bit nervous, too.

Jackson sniffed at the huge tree that had appeared in the corner of the living room. He wasn't sure what was going on, but he loved the sharp pine smell that it had. He reached up a little and nibbled the end of a branch, surprised by the spiky feel.

"Uh-uh!" Aria leaned over and gently pushed him away. "Jackson, no! It's bad for you. You'll get needles in your tummy!"

Jackson leaned against her happily, distracted by the fuss he was getting instead. His back paw drummed against the carpet as Aria scratched just the right spot behind his ear.

Aria giggled. "I love it when you do that."

"Was he eating the tree?" Mom asked, carrying in a box of decorations. Jackson got up to nose that, too. He worked his way around it, sniffing at the cardboard. What could it be?

"Just a little bit."

"Silly boy." Mom looked at the tree with a frown and called back into the hallway. "Dave, I got the decorations out of the garage, but maybe we should wait until tomorrow to put them up. It'll give the branches time to open out properly. And there's something in that puppy book about Christmas trees—it says it's good to give the dog a little while to get used to the tree before you start decorating it. That way at least, if Jackson jumps up at it, he's not going to get tangled in garland."

Dad came in from the kitchen and put down a tray on the coffee table. "Mmmm. He's definitely been a little bouncy today. He must be starting to feel Christmassy, too. We're going to have to keep an eye on him when all the family arrives. It'll be different for him with so many people in the house."

Aria looked at Jackson, who was still sniffing at the box of decorations as though it was the most interesting thing he'd ever seen. She felt a little guilty. She'd been half excited and half worried about everyone coming for Christmas, but she hadn't even thought about how Jackson was going to feel.

Jackson left the box and headed for the tray—whatever was in the mugs smelled even better. He prowled hopefully around the edge of the table, knowing he wasn't supposed to jump up.

"Hot chocolate!" Aria hurried over, and Jackson looked at her hopefully, wondering if she would share whatever the delicious-smelling stuff could be. Aria was always good at slipping him little treats….

"With marshmallows, as an end of quarter treat." Dad handed a mug to Aria. "Be careful, it's hot." Then he looked at the tree. "I hadn't thought about Jackson jumping up at the tree—isn't it cats that do that?"

"He was definitely interested in it," James said, and Jackson watched him pick up a steaming mug. Whatever it was smelled too good to miss…. "Does that mean we can't decorate the tree until tomorrow?"

"I think it's probably best, but we can do the rest of the house," Mom said. "Wrap garland around the banisters and put the wreath on the front door."

Jackson sidled closer to Aria. She had one of those good-smelling mugs now, and she was sitting on the floor. He wandered around behind her, and then came up close on her other side and ducked in for a huge slurp of hot

chocolate before she
could stop him.

"Jackson!" Aria
squeaked. "You're
so naughty!"

But Jackson
could tell
she wasn't
upset.

She was
laughing. He
licked chocolate off his damp whiskers
happily and eyed the mug. He could
try again in a minute, he figured.

"We definitely need to give him time
to get used to the tree," Mom sighed.

Chapter Two
A Full House

"They're here!" James charged to the front door with Jackson chasing excitedly after him. Aria paused the movie they'd been watching and stood up uncertainly. She wanted to go and say hello, but the hallway already had seven extra people in it, and a puppy. She would wait just a little while, until everything had calmed down.

She went to the living-room door instead, peeking around the side of it and letting the noise wash over her from a safe distance.

Jackson was bouncing up and down, twirling and whining, trying to greet all these different people. Aria heard him start to make squeaky yapping noises, too, and she went out into the hallway, gently catching his collar to stop him from jumping up. Jackson wasn't used to seeing so many new people at once, and Aria didn't want him to get too excited. Her dad had told them that Grandma was a little nervous around dogs, but Jackson was usually so gentle, they thought she would be fine with him.

"Hello, Aria! It's so good to see you."

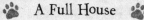

Grandma kissed Aria's cheek, and Aria hugged her. It felt like such a long time since she'd seen her grandparents, and she'd missed them. "Goodness, he's a bit, um, noisy, isn't he?" Grandma added, pulling her skirt away so Jackson's whirling tail didn't swipe it with dark hairs.

Aria sighed. That didn't seem very fair, with the noise everyone else was making. Especially Hannah, who was squealing for Grandma to look at her toy pony. Aria watched her grandma turn away from the puppy and start to fuss over her youngest grandchild. She had really hoped that Jackson would win Grandma over.

Grandpa noticed her hurt face and put an arm around her shoulders. "He's a beautiful little dog," he said, smiling. "And he's doing very well with all these strange people."

"Dad took him to training classes," Aria said proudly. "Jackson got a ribbon."

"One thing we didn't manage to teach him was to leave shoes alone, though," Dad said apologetically. "They're his favorite thing to chew, which is why we have this." He waved at the big wooden chest that stood against the wall. "Pop your shoes in there, and they'll be safe from little puppy teeth."

Uncle Josh had been bringing in all the luggage from the car, and now he stopped on the doorstep, rubbing his hands. "It's colder than ever. I think it's going to snow. A white Christmas, for once!"

"Yeah! Snowball fights!" James jumped in the air to high-five Matthew, and Aria flinched back a little. Then she looked down, smiling, as she felt Jackson lean hard against her legs. How did he always know?

Aria bent down and whispered gently to him, smoothing the fur along his back in long, slow strokes. "You're such a good boy." The little puppy nuzzled against her knees, watching the other children leaping around. "Let's try and stay out of everybody's way," she muttered. Petting Jackson was definitely making her feel less jangled up inside, and she seemed to be calming him down, too.

But everywhere that Aria and Jackson went for some peace, someone seemed to follow them. Aria's room was full of Lucy and Hannah's sleeping bags and suitcases and toys—and Lucy and Hannah. At six and three, both Aria's girl cousins were a lot younger than she was. She loved playing with them, but having them in her bedroom was just a little much, especially with Jackson, too.

"He's chasing me!" Lucy yelped, half laughing, half scared. She giggled and flapped her hands at Jackson, and Jackson yapped excitedly and tried to lick her fingers. "Oooh, he's going to bite me!"

"No, he isn't," Aria tried to explain. "Because you're sitting on the floor, he thinks you want to play."

"But I have to be on the floor. I'm trying to unpack my bag," Lucy pointed out.

Aria tried not to sigh. Lucy could unpack her bag without squeaking and wriggling and being silly, she thought. Of course, Jackson was going to try and climb all over her. "I'll take him downstairs," she said.

"No! I want to play with the puppy!" Hannah wailed. She held out a pair of sparkly garland antlers. "He can wear these!"

"I don't think he'll want to, Hannah," Aria said gently. "He doesn't really like dressing up."

"But it's Christmas! He can be a reindeer!" Hannah reached out to grab Jackson and the puppy darted away, looking up at Aria worriedly. He was friendly, but he wasn't used to people snatching at him.

"Maybe later," Aria said, hastily going out the door, with Jackson hurrying after her. She didn't really like the idea of leaving Hannah and Lucy in her bedroom, probably messing around with all of her things, but she wanted Jackson downstairs. That way, she'd have Mom and Dad to back her up if the little ones started to play with him too roughly. Dressing up as a reindeer! She could tell that Hannah thought Jackson was a real-life teddy bear, which made sense as she was only three, but Aria didn't want her upsetting him. It was Jackson's first Christmas—he should be able to enjoy it, too.

"Come on, Jackson." Aria coaxed him gently down the stairs, laughing to herself as he bounced. She never got tired of watching him hop from step to step, with his bottom waggling every time. She'd left his favorite rope chew toy in the living room, so she headed in there to find it. Jackson loved to tug on it with pretend-fierce growling noises, and Aria was sure it helped him work off his energy. With so many new people, new smells, and new things in the house, that was definitely a good idea.

All the grown-ups were sitting in the living room, chatting, and Aunt Anna turned to look at Aria and Jackson as they came in. "Oh, are the girls all right upstairs?" she asked, glancing worriedly at the ceiling. There were some thumps and squeaks coming from her bedroom.

"I think so. Lucy's unpacking their bags and Hannah's playing," Aria explained. "I just brought Jackson down here so he didn't get in their way."

"That was a good idea, Aria, thank you," Mom told her, smiling.

"Thanks, Aria." Aunt Anna reached into her handbag, which was by her feet. "I brought these for all of you children to share—why don't you put them on the Christmas tree?" She handed Aria a bag of beautiful chocolate decorations, wrapped in bright foil. Aria could smell the rich scent of chocolate rising off them as she took the bag—and if she could smell them, she was sure Jackson would be able to smell them, too.

Aria looked over at Mom and Dad, biting her lip. What was she supposed to do? They couldn't hang them on the tree—even if they were high out of Jackson's reach, he'd probably try to climb up for them.

"Oh… I'm not sure we can put them on the tree, Anna, not with Jackson around," Mom said apologetically. "I'm sorry, because it's such a sweet idea. Maybe we can use them as table decorations on Christmas Day."

Aria wasn't sure, but she thought Aunt Anna's feelings were hurt—her smile faded away. But she only nodded and said, "Okay, if that's better."

Grandma sighed and rolled her eyes, though. "Goodness, what a fuss about a little bit of chocolate."

Aria shook her head. "We're
not fussing, honestly. Chocolate's
poisonous for dogs."

"Nonsense."

Aria opened her mouth to argue—
it *wasn't* nonsense. But she caught
Mom's eye, and saw her give a tiny
shake of her head.

"Come on, Jackson," Aria whispered.
"Bring your toy. Let's find somewhere

else to play." Somehow, Christmas wasn't turning out to be quite as much fun as she'd imagined....

Jackson clambered onto Aria's lap, dangling his rope toy. He slumped down in the middle of her crossed legs and sighed. He fit perfectly, right there. He could feel the warmth of Aria seeping through into his fur, and her calmness, too. Everything was strange and loud today. The air was bright and fizzing with excitement, and for a while he'd liked it, but now he wanted to rest.

The house was full of people, and wherever he went, he seemed to be in

someone's way. One of the children
had tripped over him earlier on. He
and James had been racing through
the hallway, and the boy had stepped
on his paw. Jackson had yowled—the
boy was heavy!—and then someone
had snapped at him and told him to
be quiet. He didn't like it when people
were upset with him, and he wasn't
sure what he'd done wrong.

"It's weird, isn't it?" Aria said.
"Christmas is supposed to be a special
time, but I'm not sure I like it this
year. I don't want to spend the holiday
hiding in the laundry room, do you?"

Jackson could hear the worry in
her voice. He gave Aria's hand a very
gentle lick, and she laughed.

"You're such a good boy," she told

him, and Jackson stretched
out a little, his head
drooping over her leg.
Aria was rubbing
his ears now,
and he liked
that. It always
made him
feel sleepy.
"Maybe it
doesn't matter that we're stuck in here,"
Aria whispered, leaning down to rub
her cheek against his fur. "This is so
nice."

Chapter Three
Snow!

"Come on, Jackson," Aria said. "Time for a walk." She put her finger to her lips as Jackson began to dance around her feet with happy little whines. He knew what *that* word meant!

"Shhh," Aria whispered. "Mom said we can go out, but I don't want Hannah and Lucy to hear us. They might want to come, too. I know it's mean, but I've had enough of my little cousins, and they've only been here a day. They were the ones messing around last night, but Aunt Anna told *me* off! I don't want to get in trouble again—it's Christmas Eve!" Aria clipped on Jackson's leash and slipped quietly out the front door.

She wasn't allowed to walk Jackson on her own, but sometimes she went out with their next-door neighbor Chloe and her beautiful chocolate-spotted spaniel, Rolo. Chloe was thirteen, and she'd lived next door for as long as Aria could remember. Rolo was even older than Chloe, but he still loved his walks, although they had to be a little slow sometimes. Even before they'd had Jackson, Aria would go for walks with Chloe and Rolo. Now she could take her own puppy, too, and it felt wonderful.

"Hello! I wasn't sure you'd be able to come," Chloe called as she closed her front door and Rolo clumped down the path. "We saw all your family arriving yesterday—it looked like your house was packed!"

Aria made a face. "My cousins are everywhere. Are we going to the park? Around the lake?"

Chloe nodded. "Rolo's a little tired today—a short walk around the lake would be good."

"Jackson's going to go three times as far as Rolo anyway, running backward and forward," Aria added, grinning.

As they set off, Jackson shook himself a little, hearing his leash and collar jingle. He couldn't remember going for a walk in weather as cold as this before. The wind was slicing through his fur, and the pavement felt icy on his paws, but he didn't mind. It was exciting! It made him want to wiggle and jump and shake his ears— and he was glad to be out of the house.

Everyone seemed to be too busy to
play with him, and the rooms were
so full of people that even the air felt
strange and prickly. He knew that Aria
wasn't happy, either. He nudged his
nose against her jeans, and she leaned
down to scratch under his chin.

All the smells seemed even better than
usual this morning in the crisp, cold air.
Jackson trotted along eagerly, and he
kept looking back at Rolo, watching the
older dog plod along and hoping that
he'd hurry up. He wasn't sure why Rolo
wanted to go so slowly, but he tried his
best not to pull ahead, even though he
just wanted to get to the park.

Jackson's tail started to swish from
side to side as they reached the park
gates. He could hear the ducks in the

distance, and there was all that frosted grass to race across.... Even Rolo looked brighter, lifting his head and snuffing at the smells of the lake and the trees.

Jackson looked up hopefully at Aria, and she laughed at him. "Okay, okay. Chloe, I'm just going to run with Jackson for a little bit. He's desperate. Come on!"

Aria stepped off the path onto the grass, and Jackson barked delightedly up at the cold air as they raced along. The sky was grayish and heavy-looking, and Jackson snapped his teeth at something white that was floating down. It was cold, and strange, and it made him shiver with excitement. Another little flake of white landed on his nose, and he heard Aria calling delightedly.

"Chloe, look! It's snowing! It's really snowing!"

There was only one short flurry of snowflakes, and they soon melted away, but Jackson could feel how happy the two girls were. Aria kept trying to catch the snow on her tongue, and Chloe was laughing as the two dogs bounced around after the falling snowflakes.

Eventually Chloe called, "Let's go onto the lake. The wind's so cold—we can sit in that little shelter, and the dogs can watch the ducks for a while."

Aria nodded. "Jackson! Come on! Ducks! You know you love the ducks." She patted her leg, and Jackson trotted eagerly after her. The lake was his favorite part of the park.

Aria came back to sit in the shelter, and Jackson collapsed next to Rolo, panting a little. He'd spent a good ten minutes hurrying in and out of the trees along the bank, sniffing at old feathers and trying to stick his nose in duck poop. That was the only bad thing about walking by the lake—Jackson always seemed to find something disgusting—but at least he hadn't rolled in anything smelly.

"He has so much energy," Chloe said, laughing and leaning down to pet him.

"I know." Aria rolled her eyes. "Just imagine what it's like at my house right now with eleven people and a super-bouncy puppy."

Chloe wrinkled her nose sympathetically. "Nightmare! Although, I hate to say it, we should probably head back in a minute. I don't want Rolo to get too cold, and I promised Grandma I'd help make some pumpkin pies."

Aria sighed, and Chloe glanced at

her in surprise. "You really don't want to? Don't you have presents to wrap or anything?"

"I've done them," Aria told her. "But I guess you're right, and we should. It's just a little much at our house right now. So many cousins...."

"You have such a big family," Chloe said. She sounded a little envious, and Aria remembered something Dad had told her— that Chloe and her mom and grandma didn't have anyone else.

Aria shrugged her shoulders. "It's just that I was really looking forward to Christmas. Especially now that we have Jackson. But it's a lot, having all the family staying. I love them, but my cousins don't have a dog, and they seem to think Jackson's just a big, fluffy toy. Hannah—she's three—keeps wanting to dress him up. I mean, what would you do?"

"I don't know…." Chloe frowned. "I suppose … maybe try to put up with it—just for the holiday? They won't be staying for long, will they? And Christmas is special…. I'd definitely try to keep Jackson out of your little cousin's way, though. I bet he's not liking the idea of being dressed up."

"Yeah, that's what I'm doing." Aria

nodded. "Poor Jackson."

Chloe glanced up at the heavy gray sky, and then at Rolo, who had his tail tucked between his legs. "I'm sorry, Aria, but we should head back. Rolo looks really cold."

Aria scurried after Chloe, tugging on Jackson's leash—the puppy was still looking hopefully back over his shoulder at the ducks and geese. Was she being mean? Maybe she hadn't been welcoming enough to Lucy and Hannah and Matthew.

But Jackson kept getting into trouble just because everyone was on top of everyone else at home, and that wasn't fair. James and Matthew had really hurt him yesterday when they were racing down the hall, not looking where they were going. It *definitely* hadn't been fair for Grandma to snap at Jackson to be quiet.

Aria sighed. It was so hard to know.

She waved good-bye to Chloe and Rolo at her front door and slipped back inside. The house smelled delicious and Christmassy, like pumpkin pies, and she could hear carols playing from the radio in the kitchen. She felt her worried frown fade. Maybe she and Jackson could try to be more patient with her family. It was hard, when so many people made them both feel jumpy—but she would try.... She put on a big smile as she took off her coat and boots, and when she unclipped Jackson's leash, she whispered, "Shhh. Calm, okay? Let's be good...."

Everyone was just getting ready for lunch, and Jackson followed Aria cautiously into the kitchen. Grandpa beamed at her and kissed her on her head. "Did you have a good walk?"

Aria smiled up at him. "Yes—it even snowed a little! Did you see?"

James burst in excitedly. "Dad checked the forecast. It's going to snow even more later!" He bumped fists with Matthew, and Aria felt a bubble of excitement rise inside her.

"A real white Christmas!" she whispered to Grandpa.

As she squished into her space next to Lucy at the table, Aria felt Jackson slump down on her feet. The warm weight of him felt so good, and Lucy seemed very happy to be able to sit next to her big cousin….

Aria listened as she chatted on about her school, and her friends, and the presents she was hoping for. Then, just as Aria's mom was getting up to start the coffee and put some cookies on the table, Lucy squeaked and clutched Aria's hand. "Look! It's snowing again! There's a lot!"

Aria and the others rushed to the kitchen window, peering out excitedly. Lucy was right. It wasn't just a light flurry, like it had been earlier on. Huge flakes were floating lazily past the window—and they were already starting to stick to the grass. More and more snow came whirling down, and the lawn began to disappear under a thick white coating.

Chloe had been right, Aria decided.
It was going to be a special Christmas
after all.

Chapter Four
Jackson in Trouble

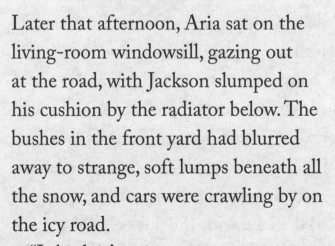

Later that afternoon, Aria sat on the living-room windowsill, gazing out at the road, with Jackson slumped on his cushion by the radiator below. The bushes in the front yard had blurred away to strange, soft lumps beneath all the snow, and cars were crawling by on the icy road.

"I think it's going to come up to our

ankles now," she said to her brother and her cousins.

"At least," James agreed, looking over the back of the couch. "I can't wait any longer—I'm going to get my boots on. Who's coming?"

All five children dashed out into the hallway to grab their things and Jackson hurried along behind, looking hopefully between them and the front door. Putting coats on usually meant a walk.

"Are you coming to look at the snow?" Aria asked Jackson as she pulled on her boots. "I hope you like it." Jackson usually loved to get wet— Aria was sure he wanted to jump right in the lake with the ducks—but a thick layer of snow was going to be very cold on his paws.

Jackson didn't seem to notice the snow right away. He shot out of the back door as he always did, excited to race around the yard with James and Matthew, who were already outside. He plunged through the thick layer of snow for the first few steps and then stopped short, staring down at the ground.

Standing in the doorway, Aria pressed her hand over her mouth, trying not to laugh.

Jackson did a strange little half jump—she'd seen him do it before, if one of his toys squeaked when he wasn't expecting it, or the time he'd tried to sniff a bumblebee. Then he looked around at Aria, his eyes open very wide.

"It's snow," Aria explained, coming out to join him. "You've never seen it before, have you? What do you think?"

Jackson put his muzzle down cautiously, sniffing at the white stuff and then giving it a little bite. Aria shivered at the thought of that sharp cold on his teeth, but he didn't seem to mind. He snuffled at the snow for a moment and then jumped back again.

Then he started to bound around the snow-covered patio, backward, while Aria watched him, giggling. "Dad! Come out here! You should take a video of this," she called. "Jackson's being so funny!"

"I want to see!" Hannah called, clumping to the back door in her coat and scarf and boots. Aunt Anna had wrapped her in so many layers that she looked almost as wide as she was tall.

Jackson was now out on the lawn with his front paws flat down and his nose pressed into the snow. He was whooshing around like a little snow plow, a flurry of white flakes flying up on either side of him. Aria was leaning against the back door, laughing so hard it almost hurt.

"He's got the zoomies," Dad said, snorting with laughter as he held up his phone to video.

"We're building a snowman," James called from farther down the yard. "Aria, come and help!"

Aria stomped out into the snow—which was already halfway up her boots—to help the boys roll a huge snowball around, and Hannah stumbled after her. Lucy lay down on her back to make a snow angel, and Jackson stopped snowplowing and watched her, fascinated.

After a little while, James and Matthew gave up on the snowman and started to hurl snowballs. Hannah squeaked and bounced around, trying to throw snowballs back and missing, and

Lucy raced across the yard to join in. Aria was reaching down for her own handful of snow when a chocolate-colored streak shot through the air beside her—it was Jackson leaping to catch one of James's snowballs. Aria had never seen him jump so high, and she gasped. She saw the puppy grab the snowball out of the air and watched it collapse into a flurry of flakes—and then Jackson landed, right on top of Hannah, knocking her down into the snow.

Hannah started to wail at once, but Matthew picked her up and started to dust the snow off her back. "You're okay! It's okay, Hannah, he didn't mean to."

"Are you all right, Hannah?" Aria gave her little cousin a hug. "Jackson was catching the snowball. Did you see him?" Hannah didn't look as though she were hurt—more just surprised.

Hannah nodded and sniffed a little, and Jackson stood there panting worriedly at her. Everything would have been fine, but then Grandma and Aunt Anna came racing out into the yard, both of them still wearing their slippers.

"Hannah!"

"Hannah, sweetie, are you all right?" Grandma turned to Aria. "What happened? What on Earth was that dog doing?"

"He didn't mean to, Grandma," James put in. "He was just leaping for the snowball I threw—it was an amazing jump. It wasn't his fault."

Aunt Anna was hugging Hannah now, anxiously patting her all over.

"He didn't hurt her—" Aria started to say.

"Didn't hurt her? He knocked her down!" Grandma snapped. "We saw it from the window!"

"Yes, but she fell in the soft snow, and she has all those layers on…." Aria really did think Hannah was okay, but the little girl started to wail now—

everyone was making so much fuss, so she was joining in.

"Dogs shouldn't be allowed near children. I told your dad, it's not safe—"

Dad came hurrying out into the yard. "Hey, Mom, don't get upset. Is Hannah all right, Anna?"

"Yes… I think so…," Aunt Anna said, but she sounded doubtful.

Jackson was still looking around uncertainly, and now he padded over to Hannah, slowly wagging his tail.

"Don't let him near her!" Grandma said, stepping in front of Hannah, and the little girl began to scream.

"No! No! Don't like it! No!"

"You see! She's terrified, Dave," Grandma said to Aria's dad. "Keep him away from her!"

Dad sighed and took hold of Jackson's collar. "Come on, Jackson, inside."

Aria stared after them, confused. Hannah had been fine! Just a little surprised. If Grandma hadn't made such a fuss, she would have kept on playing very happily. Everyone had been having fun in the snow, but now the afternoon was spoiled, and Jackson was in trouble.

Jackson padded over to the kitchen door and scratched at it, whining. He didn't understand what was going on. He hadn't been shut in the kitchen at night for weeks—he always slept upstairs now, on his cushion next to Aria's bed. He stood up on his hind paws and scratched at the door again with a whimper. Where was Aria? Why was he stuck down here? Then he caught the faint whisper of footsteps on the stairs, and his tail began to swish hopefully. Someone was coming.... He whined again, clawing eagerly at the door.

"Shhh, shhh, it's me." Aria slipped inside the door and crouched down to rub Jackson's ears and whisper to him lovingly. The little puppy wound himself around her, squeaking happily as she petted him.

"I brought my comforter," Aria whispered, tugging it through the door. "It's not fair that Aunt Anna kicked you out of my room. You didn't do anything wrong today. Grandma should never have gotten so upset. But we need to be quiet. Mom and Dad and all the grown-ups have gone to bed, but Aunt Anna and Uncle Josh are sleeping on the pull-out couch in the living room. I don't want them hearing us."

Jackson followed Aria across the kitchen uncertainly as she went to lay her comforter down by the radiator and his basket. He watched her pull the comforter around herself in a fat, fluffy sausage, and then he crept in beside her, snuggling under her arm. "Night, Jackson," Aria whispered sleepily. "It's almost Christmas."

Jackson sighed and laid his chin on his paws. He wasn't supposed to sleep on Aria's bed, although sometimes he did sneak up in the middle of the night. He loved being tucked in next to her now, but it was different. He didn't like things to be different. Why was everything suddenly so strange?

Chapter Five
Christmas Morning

"Aria!"

Aria wiggled out of her comforter, gazing sleepily back at her mom. Jackson yawned next to her and then licked her cheek. "Hey, Mom…," she mumbled. "Oh! Merry Christmas!"

"What are you doing down here?" Mom asked. She was still in her robe, and she looked bewildered rather than upset.

"Jackson was crying. I could hear him from upstairs, Mom, and it wasn't fair that he was shut down here by himself." Aria stood up, wrapping her comforter around her shoulders. "I didn't look in the stockings, I promise."

Her mom kissed the top of her head. "Oh, well. Merry Christmas! I came down to make tea for everyone. I heard James and Matthew waking up, and I was sure they'd want to be down here opening presents soon."

Aria nodded eagerly, thinking of the stockings piled on the armchair by the fireplace and the mound of presents under the Christmas tree.

"Why don't you go and get dressed? I'll feed Jackson and get breakfast ready. You can tell Lucy and Hannah that it's time for presents."

Aria hurried back upstairs. Hannah and Lucy were still asleep, but they woke up when she whispered, "It's Christmas! Come on, let's get dressed. Mom's putting some croissants in the oven, and we can do presents in a minute!" She grabbed her Christmas sweater, which had a dog in a Santa hat on it, and went to say Merry Christmas to her dad.

In the end, only the grown-ups ate the croissants. Everyone else was too excited. Hannah was standing in front of the glittering Christmas tree, staring wide-eyed at the pile of presents—there were a lot more of them than there had been yesterday.

Jackson came to stand next to her, sniffing at a large package with sparkly gold ribbons, and Hannah squeaked.

"It's fine, Hannah," Dad said soothingly. "I'm sorry, Jackson. Let's put you out in the hall for a minute. We don't want you eating the wrapping paper."

"But I have a present for him!" Aria protested. "It's his first Christmas, Dad!"

"You can give him his present later." Dad picked up the squirming puppy and carried him out into the hallway.

Uncle Josh handed the gold-ribbon package to Aria with a smile. "That one's for you, Aria, from all of us."

Of course, presents were exciting, and Aria loved hers—the gold-ribbon package had a big fluffy hoodie in it, and she got new rollerskates, and books, and a beautiful dress from Grandma and Grandpa, plus a ton of fun stuff in her stocking. But she could hear Jackson in the hallway, snuffling around and every so often letting out a tiny whimper. She knew that he didn't understand why he'd been shut out and it felt so unfair, especially when it was Christmas.

"Dad, have you seen my present for Jackson?" she asked as Dad went around with a big black bag, gathering up all the shreds of wrapping paper.

"Um, no…. What does it look like?"

"The paper had holly leaves on it." Aria kneeled on the floor and peered under the tree—there weren't any presents left. Where could it have gone?

"It probably got mixed up in someone else's pile," Mom said. "Don't worry, Aria. We'll find it in a minute. Why don't you go and try that pretty dress on?"

"Okay…." Aria nodded. She could say hello to Jackson on the way upstairs.

She went to open the door of the living room—and then she stopped, staring down at Jackson with her hand pressed against her mouth in horror.

Jackson sat in the hallway, listening to the excited noises coming from behind the door. He had been shut away from Aria and the others *again*. He hadn't even had a proper walk that morning, just a quick run around the snowy yard.

He pressed his nose against the crack between the door and the frame and sniffed sadly. He could smell the tree, and food, and people…. He put one paw up against the door and scratched, but no one came. Finally, he

wandered away from the door, thinking
he might go and curl up in his basket
in the kitchen. Or check whether he'd
accidentally left any of his breakfast.

As he padded past the big wooden
chest in the hallway, he noticed a pair
of furry winter boots tucked neatly
away underneath it. They had long,
dangly laces, with beads on the ends.
They looked interesting. Had they
been put there for him?

Jackson woofed quietly to himself
and seized one trailing bead between
his sharp puppy teeth. The string was
a thick leather, tough and delicious.
Jackson chewed all the way through
the lace in a few seconds and then
seized the boot between his front paws,
gnawing at the furry edge. He almost

forgot that he had been shut out of the living room and glanced up in surprise when Aria opened the door.

"Jackson! Oh, no!"

Jackson gazed back at her and gave his tail a worried wag. What was wrong? Why was she looking at him like that?

"What's the matter, Aria?" Mom appeared in the doorway behind her. "Oh, no. Your grandma's new boots…. Oh, he didn't…."

Aria glanced back into the living room—everyone was falling quiet.

"Um. He did…," she whispered to Mom. "What are we going to do?"

It was too late to do anything.

"My boots!" Grandma shrieked. "They're ruined! Bad dog!"

"I'm so sorry, Grandma! But Jackson didn't mean—"

"Aria, not now…," Mom said, flapping her hand in a "keep quiet" sort of way. But Aria couldn't keep quiet. Grandma hadn't been fair to Jackson from the moment she'd arrived. She just didn't like him!

"Jackson doesn't understand about not chewing things," Aria tried to explain. "That's why we have the wooden box for boots and stuff—Dad did tell everyone."

Grandma turned to look at Dad,

standing beside her with the bag of torn wrapping paper. "I don't believe this. That dog has destroyed my boots, and Aria thinks it's my fault?"

"It sort of is…," Aria said doubtfully. She hated that Grandma was so upset—but it *was* her fault. Or at least, it definitely wasn't Jackson's.

"Aria!" Mom snapped. "I told you to be quiet, now stop it. Dave, I think we'd better put Jackson in the laundry room and out of the way."

Aria blinked, her eyes suddenly hot with tears. She was only saying what had happened, and now *she* was getting scolded, and Jackson had to be shut away again. Grandma was the one who hadn't listened to Dad. Why was everyone being so mean?

Chapter Six
A Christmas Walk

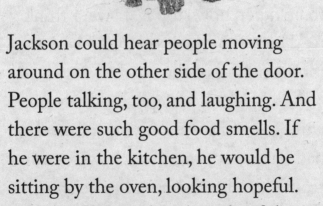

Jackson could hear people moving around on the other side of the door. People talking, too, and laughing. And there were such good food smells. If he were in the kitchen, he would be sitting by the oven, looking hopeful.

He sniffed hard at the side of the door and then padded sadly back to his basket. He had his toys, and one of them even had treats hidden inside the holes, but he hadn't bothered to try to nibble them free. He wanted to be out there with everyone else. Even if no one gave him any of that delicious-smelling food, he would still be with them. He liked being part of things. This little room was lonely and sad.

He didn't really understand what had gone wrong. Aria had looked at those furry boots, and then her voice had turned strange. She had been frightened, he thought. But the boots had just been sitting there, the dangling strings like a toy—like something he was supposed to chew. Why had they been there if they weren't for him to play with? It was wrong…. Everything was wrong.

Aria stood by the door to the laundry room. She could hear Jackson inside, his claws tapping on the tile floor as he paced back and forth. She pressed her hand against the door, biting her bottom lip. Jackson was missing his first Christmas. She hadn't even given him his present, and no one seemed to care that she couldn't find it.

"Aria, don't disturb him," Dad said gently. "If we leave him alone, he'll probably settle down and go to sleep."

"I wasn't disturbing him. I'm just …
missing him. Can't we take him for a
walk? He hasn't been out today."

"It's too cold, surely." Mom looked
around from the oven. "He won't want
to walk in all this snow."

"I don't think he'd mind. Just a
short walk. To the lake and right back
again?"

"Well, I can't go," Mom said shortly.
"I'm trying to cook Christmas dinner
for eleven people, Aria. And your dad's
helping. Jackson's going to have to
wait, I'm afraid."

Aria looked meaningfully toward
the hallway and the living room—full
of people who could help with the
cooking, or even go with her to take

Jackson for a walk.

"Go and see if Grandpa wants to go with you," Dad suggested, and Aria nodded eagerly. But when she peeked round the living-room door—she was still avoiding Grandma—Grandpa was snoozing comfortably on the couch. Aria wasn't actually sure how he could manage it, since James and Matthew were trying to teach Grandma how to play Matthew's new video game, and there was a lot of yelling going on. But Aria didn't want to disturb him.

"He's asleep," she reported gloomily to Dad. "Aunt Anna's taking care of Lucy and Hannah, and Uncle Josh and Grandma and James are playing Matthew's new game with him."

"We'll go for a walk later, Aria," Dad

said. "Jackson won't mind waiting a little while."

Just then, Jackson whined and scratched at the door. Dad sighed. "He heard me say his name, I suppose. Bella, how about if Aria and I take him out quickly?"

"No one's set the table yet," Mom pointed out, rubbing her hot face with the oven mitts.

"Oh, I'd forgotten about that…. Okay, Aria, you can take Jackson for a quick walk around the block on your own. Just this once." He patted Mom's hand when she looked worried. "They'll be fine. They aren't going far."

"Yes!" Aria went to hug Dad. "Thank you! We'll be really good."

Aria hurried out into the hall again

to fetch her things and Jackson's leash,
and wrapped herself in her coat, fluffy
hat, and a big scarf. Then she carefully
opened the laundry-room door, in case
Jackson dashed out and went to throw
himself all over Grandma.

He didn't. The puppy was sitting
in his basket, looking worried, and he
didn't move until Aria went to kneel
down next to him.

"Hey," she whispered. "What's up,
Jackson?"

The puppy pressed his nose gently into her hand, and his tail thumped against the basket, but he still didn't leap up happily the way he usually would if he thought he was going for a walk.

"You don't know what's going on, do you?" Aria asked. "You missed your walk, and then you got shut away on your own.... I'm sorry, Jackson. Come on, I promise we're going for a walk now. I mean it. A special Christmas walk! Come on!"

Jackson's tail swished faster, and when he saw that Aria had his leash, he bounced up, squeaking and wiggling with excitement. Aria let out the breath she'd been holding as she clipped on the leash. She hated that he'd been so confused.

"See you in a bit," she told her
parents as they made for the back door.

"Just around the block, Aria!" Mom
called after them, and Aria waved to
show she'd heard. The side path was
almost clear of snow—it was sheltered
by the wall—but the front yard
was covered. Snow had fallen again
overnight, covering up the footprints
from the day before. Hardly anyone
had been out, since it was Christmas
Day, and the whole street looked like
something from a Christmas card.
As they padded carefully onto the
pavement, the sun started to come
out, and the snow glittered brightly.
It was so fresh that it crunched under
Aria's boots.

"Your tummy's going to get cold," Aria said to Jackson, watching him bounce through the thick snow. It was almost up to the top of the puppy's legs, and it was hard for him to walk through—he was moving in little jumps instead, sinking down into the snow each time. Aria had expected him to leave a trail of pawprints, but Jackson was plowing a channel through instead. He seemed to be enjoying it, though—his tongue was hanging out, and Aria could feel him pulling eagerly on the leash.

"You really did need a walk," she said. "It's so beautiful—it feels like we're the only people out here at all. Oh, look at the tree!" Aria loved the huge chestnut at the end of their street.

It had tall pink candle flowers in the springtime, and then it dropped glossy nuts just about the time they went back to school after the summer. Now it was black against the gray-white sky, each branch lacy with a fine layer of snow.

Jackson was making for the edge of the pavement—not that they could see it very easily—aiming to cross the street and head left to the park, and the lake, but Aria tugged gently on his leash. "No, we have to go this way today." She sighed. "I know. I want to go to the lake, too—I bet it's all frozen over now! But Mom and Dad said just around the block."

They turned right instead, Aria admiring the strange new yards, all snowy humps and bumps, and the Christmas lights washing bright colors across the snow. But all too soon they were walking back along their own road. Aria saw Jackson realize where they were and his ears sag down.

"I'm sorry, Jackson," she whispered. "It wasn't long enough, was it?" Aria looked at her watch. There was still a while until Christmas dinner. Mom and Dad wouldn't be worrying; they were much too busy. "We could go around the block again," Aria said, crouching down to brush some of the loose snow off Jackson's fur. "Or … it isn't that far to the park, I guess. Nobody's going to know, and they don't want you in the house, do they?" She blinked hard, thinking about having to shut Jackson in the laundry room again, all by himself. "No one's going to miss me, either. Grandma's still upset—it's like she thinks I *gave* you her boots! We'd be doing everyone a favor by staying out of the way...."

Aria glanced around guiltily and nodded to herself. "We won't be long," she whispered. Then she hurried across the street, Jackson trotting happily beside her.

Chapter Seven
Trouble at the Park

Jackson pressed against Aria's legs,
closing his eyes as the wind cut
through his wet fur. It hadn't been this
cold when they set out, he was sure. He
looked back across the wide, wet sheet
of snow that had covered his park and
shivered. There was a thin, grayish
line snaking through the snow behind
him—where he'd fought for every step.

He'd been desperate for a walk, but
now it felt as if they were
a very long way from
home.

"Oh, Jackson."
Aria sounded
worried, and he
gave his tail the
smallest of wags
as he looked up
at her. "You look so
cold. Maybe we shouldn't have come
this far." She crouched down in the
snow, rubbing at his soaked coat with
her gloves. It was nice, but it didn't
make him feel much warmer. "I've got
an idea. Come on. We're almost at the
lake. We can go and sit in the shelter
out of the wind for a while and warm

up. Then you'll feel better. And look what I've got...." She reached into her coat pocket and pulled out a crinkling packet. Jackson brightened at once. He recognized that noise—Aria had treats! "I knew you'd like them. They were in my pocket. It's not exactly Christmas dinner, but they'll do. Come on, let's run. It'll warm us both up."

Jackson galloped after Aria. The thought of the dog treats had given him new energy, and he went bounding over the snow in huge puppy leaps. He hardly even noticed the ducks huddled around the icy lake because he was too eager to get to the shelter and beg for those treats from Aria.

"It's definitely warmer in here," Aria said as they ducked inside. "Wow,

the lake looks really frozen— it has
snow on top of it. I've never seen it
like that before." Then she shuddered
and squeaked, "Ooooh, Jackson!" as he
shook himself briskly, flinging off the
icy meltwater. Jackson looked around,
surprised, not sure what he'd done.

"Never mind. I have a coat and
you don't. Here." Aria leaned down,
and Jackson squirmed in her arms as
she lifted him onto the bench. She
unwound her fluffy scarf and wrapped
it around him tightly, so only his head
stuck out. "There, that'll warm you up
a bit. Purple's definitely your color,"
she told him. Jackson wiggled, snorting
uncertainly at the scarf. He wasn't
sure about it being tucked around his
paws, but it did make him feel warmer.

"Okay, I'm getting the treats."

Jackson nudged hopefully at Aria's coat—he could smell the food even through the foil packet. He stood up, the scarf sliding away as Aria started to feed him the little meaty sticks. Jackson gobbled them down happily, forgetting about his cold paws and wet fur.

"All gone." Aria held out her hands to him. "You've had them all."

Jackson stuck his nose into the packet hopefully, but it was definitely empty. He sighed and slumped down on the bench next to Aria, gazing out at the icy lake. It was still cold, but he didn't care—he'd much rather be out here with Aria than shut in the laundry room back at home.

Aria leaned against the wooden wall of the shelter with a sigh. Jackson had scrambled down from the bench now and was sniffing curiously underneath it. She checked her watch. Just a couple more minutes sheltering from the cold wind, and then they'd set off for home again. Mom and Dad might have noticed they weren't back—but it was only a ten-minute walk. Maybe a little longer, fighting their way through the snow.

The thing was, Aria still didn't really want to go home. She'd been looking forward to this Christmas so much—doing all the fun things her family usually did, but now with a puppy, too! Except it hadn't worked out that way. No one seemed to want Jackson around. Why have a puppy, Aria thought miserably, if all they did was push him away?

There was a sharp tug on the leash, and Aria looked up in surprise. Jackson had stopped snuffling in the dust under the bench. Instead, he was straining hard on the leash, staring at a pair of ducks waddling toward the lakeside.

"No, you can't chase them—" Aria started to say, but just then, the ducks seemed to notice that Jackson was watching them, and they went into a panic. They flapped wildly, half running, half flying toward the frozen lake, and Jackson began to bark with excitement. He yanked hard on the leash, so hard that he dragged it out of Aria's hand and shot after them.

"Jackson, no!" Aria yelled, reaching down for the end of the leash—but Jackson was moving too quickly. It slid along the ground, just too fast for Aria to grab it.

The two ducks dashed out onto the snow-covered ice, quacking angrily, their webbed feet slipping in the snow. Jackson bounded after them. He probably didn't even realize he was heading out onto the lake, Aria thought, her heart thumping hard in her throat as she hurried after him. It was almost impossible to see where the bank and the water joined—there were just a few brownish reeds sticking up out of the snow.

"Jackson!" Aria called. "Come here,

boy, come here!" But Jackson was too focused on the ducks to listen to her. She could see it. They were practically in front of his nose, and the way they were flapping and squawking was driving him wild with excitement. He bounced around on the snowy ice, never actually getting anywhere near the ducks, but loving the chase.

Aria grabbed a branch that was poking out of the snow, hauling it up like a walking stick. She needed to get closer to Jackson, to get him to listen, but she didn't know how thick the ice was. Could she stand on it? It seemed thick enough to hold up the ducks and Jackson, but what about a person? She couldn't even see where the ice started....

"Jackson, please come back...." If only she hadn't already fed him all the dog treats. Aria jabbed carefully at the snow with her stick, trying to figure out where was bank and where was lake. But then she looked up sharply. Was that a crack? It was only faint ... just a little snapping noise.... Or had she imagined it? It was hard to tell with Jackson barking and the ducks still quacking in panic.

"Jackson!" Aria screamed. "Jackson, come here!"

Jackson glanced back at Aria across the snow-covered lake. The ducks had flown away to the other side,

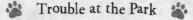

quacking furiously. Jackson eyed them,
disappointed. They had been fun to
chase, with all that flapping. Was Aria
going to throw that stick? He looked
at her hopefully and barked. Then he
scampered across the ice toward her
and barked again, bouncing up and
down and watching the stick.

"Jackson, no! Oh, don't do that!"
Aria cried. "Jackson, the ice is cracking!
Please come here, come on, quick!"

Jackson shook himself, confused. What was the matter with Aria? Why did she sound so upset again? This was a good game. He liked to fetch, and usually Aria would throw him sticks or a ball in the yard for a long time. He didn't understand that frightened squeak in her voice.

Jackson swished his tail uncertainly, gazing across the lake at Aria and wondering what to do. He whined— and then the ice cracked underneath his paws, and his whine turned into a terrified whimper.

Chapter Eight
The Perfect Christmas

Aria kneeled down on the snowy
edge of the bank, stretching the stick
in front of her. Jackson was standing
there, a few feet out on the snow-
covered ice. She could see him shaking.
How did he suddenly look so much
smaller?

There were cracking sounds all
around them now—the lake had

looked so solid only minutes ago, but the ice could only be a few inches thick after all. Jackson was looking down at his paws in horror, and Aria realized that it wasn't just him shaking—it was the ice, breaking apart and wobbling under his feet.

"Jackson," she whispered, her voice wobbling, too. She pushed the stick out as far as she could, but there was still about three feet to go. The puppy couldn't reach it, not without stepping forward, and then he might go through the ice into the freezing water.

If he fell in, Aria wasn't sure she'd ever be able to get him out.

She pulled the stick back in and jabbed hard at the snowy ice just in front of her. It seemed solid. Really solid and thick. And the lake couldn't be that deep right at the edge, could it? Aria closed her eyes for a moment, and then she opened them again and smiled reassuringly at Jackson. "It's okay. I'm coming. You stay there."

She'd read a book about someone being rescued off a frozen river before. You had to spread your weight—that was the important thing. Shivering, she eased herself down flat onto the ice, stretching out long and thin, and pushing the stick as far forward as she could. But would Jackson understand what to do? Would the stick even reach far enough for him to grab?

Aria gasped as she saw Jackson sniff at the end of the stick. "Yes...," she whispered. "That's it, Jackson. Bite it! Bite it, and I can pull you back. Come on...."

But Jackson didn't seem to know what she wanted. He just kept sniffing at the stick and then looking hopefully at Aria, as though he wanted her to come and get him.

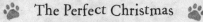

Maybe she should? If she stretched out carefully, couldn't she wiggle a little farther onto the ice? She was just starting to edge closer toward Jackson when he decided to come to her instead. He didn't grab on to the stick, he just padded toward her—and then, with a yelp, he went through the ice and into the freezing lake.

"No!" Aria screamed, watching him paddle desperately to keep his nose above the dark water. "Jackson, the stick, grab the stick!" She pushed it sideways, and this time, Jackson bit down hard. "Yes! Oh, good boy, good boy!" Aria started to slide herself backward, pulling Jackson up out of the water. It seemed to take forever, but at last she pulled the soaked, shivering puppy onto the ice again. "Don't let go," she told him, still wiggling toward the bank. They must be almost there.

Aria felt her feet nudge against the bank, and she gasped in relief. They were almost safe, as long as they could get back onto solid ground without the ice cracking under them again.

Then she felt someone grab her firmly around the waist and a gloved hand closed over hers, pulling the stick back toward the bank. Dad lifted her off the ice and set her down on the snow-covered grass, hugging her tightly.

"Jackson…," Aria cried, struggling in his arms.

"Mom's got him. It's okay, Aria. He's here—look." Dad spun her to face the lake again so she could see Jackson shivering next to her and Mom pulling off her scarf to wrap around him.

"You got him out, Aria. He was practically on the bank by the time I grabbed him," Mom said, her voice shaking. "Why were you on the ice? You could have gone through so easily!"

"I had to rescue him," Aria said, in a very small voice. "I was only just at the edge, Mom. I couldn't leave him. It was my fault. I wasn't holding the leash tightly enough, and he saw some ducks and tried to chase them. He didn't know the ice wasn't safe."

"But *you* did, and you still went out on it," Dad said grimly. "You can't do anything like that again, Aria, not ever. You scared us so much. When we saw you lying on the ice… I was just waiting for it to give way under you." He was holding her so tightly, Aria could hardly breathe.

"I wasn't going to leave him," Aria whispered. "How could I? No one's taken care of him all Christmas, not even me."

"What do you mean?" Mom asked.
"Tell us while we're walking. We need
to get you two back in the warm house."
She was holding Jackson in her arms,
but he still looked cold and miserable.

"It isn't his fault that Grandma
and Hannah don't like dogs," Aria
explained, her words stumbling over
each other. "He's not used to having
so many people around. He's only a

puppy, and everything's new for him! But he's the one who keeps getting shut away in the laundry room. And he wasn't allowed to sleep in my room like he usually does. People shouted at him when he didn't know what he'd done wrong. And then he wasn't even going to get a walk!"

"Except he did," Mom pointed out. "Because we let you go out, and we trusted you to go just around the block. You knew that's what we'd said, Aria, didn't you?"

"Yes," Aria muttered. "But it wasn't fair."

"No…." Dad squeezed her shoulders tightly. "No, all right. It wasn't fair."

"Really?" Aria looked up at him in surprise.

"Mm-hmm. We didn't take care of him properly, I can see that. I'm sorry. But sometimes things aren't fair, Aria. I know you were trying to make things better for Jackson, but you didn't do it the right way. You should have talked to us."

"I tried to!"

Jackson wiggled in Mom's arms, trying to lick Aria's face, and Mom sighed. "We just wanted to keep everyone happy, Aria. It's difficult, with a houseful of people. I didn't realize how hard it would be for a puppy, having everyone here for Christmas. We should have thought about it more."

"I'm sorry we went to the park," Aria said. She was leaning against her dad's side, and he was so warm. She was starting to feel a little bit better, now that Mom and Dad were listening to her. "It's just … it felt like no one wanted us back at home very much. I didn't think you'd notice," she added in a whisper, watching her mom's face fall.

"Aria!" Mom sounded horrified.

"Your mom had the minutes counted," Dad told her. "When you'd been gone ten minutes, she kept going to the door to check where you were. By twenty minutes she had her coat on, and she'd left Aunt Anna in charge of

Christmas dinner. We should hurry up and get back—I don't think Anna was very happy about it. I'll call her now and let her know we're on our way."

"Christmas dinner isn't the end of the world," Mom said crossly. "We shouldn't have let you go out on your own in the first place. I should have made your dad go with you and gotten Uncle Josh and James and Matthew to help set the table. And this afternoon, if Jackson feels up to another walk, we'll all go."

"Although that might mean my mom having to wear those poor boots," Dad said, grinning. "It might not be popular…."

"Aria, look!"

Aria blinked at her little cousin and realized that she'd been dozing on the couch. Jackson was definitely asleep, slumped over her lap, still half wrapped in the towel Mom had used to dry him when they got home. Falling in a lake made you tired, Aria decided.

It wasn't even lunchtime yet, but the whole house smelled like turkey. Jackson was going to have some fancy dog food that was meant to taste like Christmas dinner. Mom had bought it for him specially when she did the Christmas food shopping. Aria thought he might have preferred the real thing, but it was the thought that mattered. She loved it that Mom had planned a treat just for Jackson.

When they'd gotten back from the park, the whole family seemed to be crowded into the hallway, staring at her and Jackson, and Aria had huddled up close to Mom. She'd been expecting Grandma to tell her off for going to the park and getting into trouble. But Grandma had hugged her instead, and she'd looked really worried.

Aunt Anna had told Lucy and Hannah to move their toys off the couch so that Aria and Jackson could sit down, and no one had said anything about wet dogs on the furniture….

"What is it?" she asked Hannah now, trying not to yawn.

"I found your present! You lost it, and I found it!" Hannah shoved a package under Aria's nose, the gold paper scattered with tiny holly leaves.

"Be gentle, Hannah," Grandpa said, leaning over from the armchair.

"Oh! Jackson's present! Where was it?"

"Under the couch." Hannah looked very pleased with herself. "I found it! Can we open it now?"

Aria smiled at her. "It's for Jackson, though. He's asleep."

"Oh…." Hannah looked disappointed.

"You could help him open the present when he wakes up," Aria suggested, and her little cousin nodded eagerly. She squashed herself in between Jackson and the arm of the couch and leaned against Aria.

She was desperate to wake Jackson up, Aria could tell, but she was trying very hard not to. Luckily, after a couple more minutes, the puppy snuffled a little and then sneezed, surprising himself awake. He nosed at Hannah and then licked her hand, making her giggle.

"Look, Jackson. You got a present." Hannah held it out to him hopefully and then added, "Let's open it!" She started to rip at the paper and Jackson leaned forward curiously, sniffing at the package.

"Oooooh," Hannah said, pulling out a Christmas tree toy. "Pretty tree!" She glanced uncertainly at Aria, and then at Jackson, who was giving the tree a hopeful look.

"I think he wants to chew it," Aria explained. "That's what it's for. And it has more toys inside, see? That little candy cane? He has to try and get them out. It's so he doesn't get bored."

Hannah nodded and pushed the tree gently toward Jackson. He sniffed it and then poked his nose curiously into the hole in the side. He popped back out with a little stocking-shaped toy in his teeth, and Hannah burst out laughing.

"I think he likes it," Aria said, giggling, too. She rubbed the puppy's soft fur, and Hannah copied her carefully.

"He's very patient with her," Grandma said, coming to sit on Aria's other side. She still sounded a little bit surprised, but Aria smiled at her anyway and nodded. She could tell Grandma was trying to be nice. "I've never had a dog, Aria," Grandma went on slowly. "I don't know very much about them. I shouldn't have been so upset with him yesterday."

"It's okay, Grandma...."

"Would he let me pet him?"

Grandma asked. She was nervous, Aria realized.

"I think he'd love it," she said, trying to sound encouraging, and Grandma gently patted the top of Jackson's head.

"Good dog…," she said, and Aria beamed at her, and then at Grandpa, too. Jackson *was* a good dog. He looked so happy, with Grandma and Hannah fussing over him while he chewed on his special Christmas toy.

Jackson glanced up at her and thumped his tail slowly against her leg. He wiggled a little, shoving his new toy closer, as if he wanted to share it with her, and then he yawned.

Aria looked down at him lovingly. This was just what she'd wanted for Christmas.

HOLLY
WEBB

Holly Webb started out as a children's book editor and wrote her first series for the publisher she worked for. She has been writing ever since, with more than 100 books to her name. Holly lives in England, with her husband, three children, and several cats who are always nosing around when she is trying to type on her laptop.